HATTIE PEARL
CLICK CLICK

by

Emily Hearn

Illustrations by

Yvonne Cathcart

SECOND
STORY
Press

CANADIAN CATALOGUING IN PUBLICATION DATA

Hearn, Emily, date
Hattie Pearl click click

ISBN 0-929005-44-9

1. Cathcart, Yvonne.   11. Title
PS 8565.E37H38 1993   jC813'.54   C93-093737-6
PZ7.H33Ha   1993

Second Story Press gratefully acknowledges
the assistance of the Ontario Arts Council and the Canada Council

Printed and bound in Canada

Published by
SECOND STORY PRESS
760 Bathurst St.
Toronto Canada M5S 2R6

*for Shurly Dickson
and my brother, Bill Wadley
and our families, with love*

I feel myself rising ... being lifted up ... up ... up ... I'm sailing through fluffy clouds ... Oh no! Hot sparks are shooting up at me ... I'm flying over a flaming volcano ... Yipe! I'm being sucked down! ...

"Janey, JANEY. SUPPER!" That's Elsie, my older sister.

I scramble off my flying carpet near the willow tree. The edges did — they DID curl up!

"AND BRING THAT OLD RUG WITH YOU. IT'S GOING TO RAIN."

"I'M COMING RIGHT NOW," I yell, dragging my carpet across the grass. Too bad it couldn't fly me right through our back door, right to my place at the table. Elsie would faint, probably. Mum and Dad would laugh and roar. So would Hattie Pearl, the girl from the country who was renting a room in our house.

It's a long time now since I was that skinny little day-dreaming kid. I made up stories, even in school. It was more fun than learning to read, which wasn't as easy for me as it seemed to be for Elsie. Words that were big black specks to me she could read right away, quick as a fox.

Why like a fox? Well, a typing exercise in those days went "the quick brown fox jumps over the lazy dog." Hattie Pearl had a filing job at the insurance company in town; but she wanted to earn more money being a secretary, so she'd practise on our big old typewriter. I'd hear her through my bedroom wall muttering about the fox, while THUMP, THUMP, THUMP, she'd clunk the heavy keys, slowly, over and over again.

"Aren't you fed up with the fox and that dumb dog?" I asked her one night.

Hattie Pearl winked, "Can you think of anything better?"

"Sure. A green mosquito would be more fun. It could zing around a baby elephant. Or maybe an orange turtle could flop about in snowshoes. Or ..."

"That's enough," said Mum, and Elsie rolled her eyes. "Tell me later," Hattie Pearl laughed in her funny way.

When I went to her room after supper she listened to every word of the stories I'd been making up on the magic carpet. They were stories I hadn't told anyone else. I could have gone on the whole night.

But Mum came to the door. "Time for bed," she said. "You have to be up for school, don't forget."

School. How could I forget it? School meant reading, and all those black squiggles that shifted on pages when I wanted to make sense of them!

"Goodnight, Hattie Pearl," I sighed. "See you at breakfast."

While I was pulling up the quilts I heard the familiar THUMP THUMP start up, then the sound of her voice. But what was she saying? Was it "a green mosquito zinged around a baby elephant?" Yes, it really was! It was my own chant, over and over, lulling me to sleep.

It was my job in the morning to take the neighbour's kids to nursery school. As I walked hand in hand with Denny and Hazel I'd invent a secret life for the white dog who slept in the fenced yard at our corner. Now *there* was a lazy dog.

I told them that we always saw it asleep because at night it was wide awake. And it wasn't a dog any more. It had changed into a unicorn. If they could touch the spot between its eyes they'd feel the tip of a white horn that grew after dark. Wings would fan out from its sides as it rose in the air over our rooftops ... over the schools ... higher than the highest tree ... far above the clouds. Its call was a soft neigh on the nightwind.

When they asked I told them that the unicorn had a special umbrella for when it rained, and no, it didn't take any passengers. When we saw it twitching and snoring it might be dreaming of the games it played with other creatures among the stars.

What kind of creatures? Ideas for new ones popped into my head each day. Maybe a silver whale that spouted meteors as it swam through the sky. Or shimmery birds that sang haunting songs as they soared. Or monkeys that turned endless cartwheels through space.

I never for a single second thought Denny and Hazel believed any of my stories.

Next day, after my usual struggle with the teacher and mixed-up words, Hattie Pearl proudly handed me a sheet of paper covered with typing.

"This is for you, Jane. I typed a whole story! It's the one you told me about your magic carpet almost landing inside a volcano."

How could I tell her that I couldn't even read it? She looked puzzled that I wasn't happy to see my own story looking as if it were printed in a real book. But I was so bewildered that I didn't even thank her.

Somehow Hattie Pearl caught on. Taking back the page, she just smiled and said, "If I was up half the night trying to type this, I guess I can help its author learn to read it. Why don't you come in and work with me after supper?"

Work? At NIGHT? I didn't like that idea much, but she was such fun to be with that I agreed.

I worked all right. From then on, night after night, PLUNK, DUNK, SLUNK ... FLIP, SLIP, PLIP ... BOO, HOO, MOO ... we'd pick word patterns and then we'd create more. We'd chant them, sing them, scream them. Elsie played the piano loudly so she couldn't hear us.

In these new stories my carpet flew to different, exciting lands. It rose, drifted, and landed in everything from molasses to thistles, from slippery ice to dark, smelly tunnels, from outer space to tangled jungles.

We ran into woolly bears, scaley dragons, big-bellied giants, and mechanical toys that moved by themselves. Sometimes we dropped in on squeaky humans, so tiny they lived in seashells and sandcastles left behind by children on tide-beaches.

Hattie Pearl practised typing my tales, trying to do them without a mistake the very first time. I'd slave away reading one and when I could do it smoothly she'd give me the perfect copy to keep. I'd add it to the folder I kept in my dresser. Was it ever getting fat! It was almost as thick as the red sweater that lay on top.

Summer holidays weren't far off. And now, my teacher
was pleased with me. Words weren't such a speckled jum-
ble any more. I overheard her say to my mother that reading "just takes some children longer than others."

"It's just that Hattie Pearl helps me!" I wanted to shout.
Hattie Pearl's typing was fast now. My bedtime lullabies
weren't thumps any more, but lively clicketyclicketyCLICKS.

The frolics of the unicorn were coming to an exciting end. I told Denny and Hazel that it would be spending its vacation with the sky creatures in an enchanted playground at the back of the moon.

"NOW YOU'VE DONE IT, JANE, TELLING ALL THOSE LIES!"

"LIES?"

What did Elsie mean now?

"Denny broke his arm climbing the fence to get to old Whitey. What made you say he's a unicorn?"

Denny BELIEVED me?

Poor Denny. How his arm must hurt.

And it was all my fault. I cried and cried and Mum held me tight.

"You know, Janey, we'll have to go over and tell him how sorry we are."

"I will," I snuffled "but Mum, those weren't lies. They were my stories. I was just making things exciting on that same old trip every day."

"I know that. But Denny couldn't understand. He's only three years old."

When I didn't have any tears left I started thinking. What could I do to help Denny feel better? The instant I saw Hattie Pearl coming home from work I knew what it had to be. I told her I wanted to give Denny my stories even though they were the only copies there would ever be. We didn't have photocopiers in those days. She agreed that it was a gift he'd like.

If we put the stories together to look like a book he'd know that everything I'd written was make-believe.

Hattie Pearl helped me find stiff cardboard and shiny wrapping paper to make the covers. We punched holes and tied it with my fanciest hair ribbon.

Later, when I finally sat beside Denny and read him the first story about the volcano, he got all fired up. He wanted to make pictures to go with it. He had a great time splashing paint and crayoning on extra paper that we added. Right away my flying carpet had become his too.

I signed his cast for him. He pulled me to him and whispered "Janey, draw Whitey unicorn beside your name." And I did.

By the time school was over Denny's arm was almost better. Hattie Pearl got the job she wanted and moved out to share an apartment with her girlfriend. Our family went away to my uncle's farm.

When we went for walks and passed the vegetable patch I'd tell them the adventures I was making up about the scarecrow. It looked as if it were just standing there, but ...

"You know what, Janey," Mum said one afternoon, "I bet you're going to be a writer."

"You know what," I replied, thinking of Denny's book, "I already am!"

And we were right. I began by scribbling my poems and stories. Then I learned to type them. And now I send them to publishers on my speedy computer.

Writing has become my career. Children who like my work often want to share their stories with me. And they do it by modem, on computers in their schools.

It's like magic. When I tap the computer key twice — click click — quick as a fox, their terrific ideas come up on my screen. Before I reply, I have to type my password. It's supposed to be a secret, but if you haven't already guessed, I'll tell you what mine is.

It's the name of that wonderful, long-ago girl who helped me learn to read and kept my imagination flying. Each time before I tap the quick click click, I type:

HATTIE PEARL.